About the Author

Madison Stagner is a high school English teacher in the United States. She grew up in Virginia and has always enjoyed writing and reading. She received a double bachelor's degree in Creative Writing, and Language and Literature at Virginia Polytechnic Institution and University in Blacksburg, Virginia. She then received her Master's in Teaching at James Madison University in Harrisonburg, Virginia. Madison is an avid reader and writer, who encourages her students' passion for English through various writing workshops and exciting approaches to reading in the English classroom.

Ambush

Madison Stagner

Ambush

Olympia Publishers
London

www.olympiapublishers.com
OLYMPIA PAPERBACK EDITION

A CIP catalogue record for this title is
available from the British Library.

ISBN: 978-1-80439-202-7

This is a work of fiction.
Names, characters, places and incidents originate from the writer's
imagination. Any resemblance to actual persons, living or dead, is
purely coincidental.

First Published in 2023

Olympia Publishers
Tallis House
2 Tallis Street
London
EC4Y 0AB

Printed in Great Britain

Dedication

I dedicate this book to my grandfather, Edward Lee Stagner, the most hardworking, loving, and strong-willed man I ever had the pleasure to call family. I love you more than words could ever tell. Thank you for being such a role model to me and others.

Acknowledgements

I would like to say thank you to my mother, father, grandmother, grandfather, and nana, who have always believed in me and supported me through writing this story. I know that it is because of the faith and love of you all that these pages came to be.

"Luke," Edward said, "let's play soldier."

He knew instantly that Luke's blue eyes would be looking up at him, a smile playing at the edges of his mouth, excitement flooding through his body. He rarely asked Luke to play soldier. That was in part because Luke was Edward's younger brother. A younger brother he particularly enjoyed bossing around.

Usually, he'd shove off some chore he didn't want to do but today was different. He wanted to show Luke he is not all bad. Plus, he knew these were the times that made all the others bearable, what gave Luke the energy to do what he told him to. The days where he sat next to him on the wooden bench their father had built. The bench where they were the men of the house. The bench where every once in a blue moon, Edward asked Luke to play.

"Really?" Luke prodded.

"Yeah," Edward said. He slapped Luke's back. "Go grab your gun and I'll tell Mom we'll be back for dinner."

Luke nodded rapidly before he bounded toward the house and squeezed through the door.

Luke pressed past their mother as she brought out the laundry. She tumbled a little as he knocked her basket loose from her grip. She smiled to herself, adjusted the basket, and walked towards the clothesline. Her eyes crawled the banked backyard to find Edward and he grinned.

"What're the plans for today?" she yelled.

"We're gonna go play soldier in the woods!"

"Oh, very fun!" She nodded. "Just be careful, okay, Honey?"

Edward chuckled. "Always!"

Her eyes softened at him, and warmth from them

radiated in his heart. He loved her more than words could explain and a smile tugged his lips as he watched her set the basket gently onto the concrete porch.

His father leaving every few weeks for work had pushed them into growing closer. To manage the household, Edward and his mother worked together. They had never been as close as they were now.

Edward did his part by collecting firewood, bringing home squirrels and rabbits, and washing the dishes a few nights a week. It wasn't much, but his mother appreciated the help and he enjoyed feeling useful. Most of the time.

His mom was a particular woman. She preferred things to be done in a specific manner. Shirts folded after being hung in the sun to dry *must* be folded with shoulders tucked in and split at the half. Pants *must* be bent at the crotch seam and folded into quarters.

The few nights he did the dishes, she would hover to ensure they were washed as thoroughly as she liked. A small, amused huff escaped his lips as she crouched to swat imaginary dirt from the top of her moccasins. "Eddie, don't give me that look," she always said, "you know cleanliness is close to Godliness."

He smirked, the moccasins were spotless but away she wiped.

He shrugged. They were new, so he maybe he could understand the overprotective sense of determination. *These* will be the pair that you take care of. *These* will be the shoes you keep clean.

His dad had bought and brought them from Iowa on his last haul and his mom was bound and determined to keep those puppies clean.

He shook his head as he stood and walked down the hill. The breeze brushed against his face and pulled playful at his t-shirt. He relished the feeling; it was a perfect late-summer day.

The sky was painted a clear, bluebird hue, and the grass a faded mint. The chilled wisps of air that swam in the wind, though welcomed, held their warning for fall, but he didn't care. The warmth of summer was still strong, and he knew he'd have at least another month before autumn truly took over.

"Honey?" she hollered loudly, crouching to pick her first piece of clothing from the basket. "Y'all need to be..."

"Back before dark. I know," Edward said.

With a gasp, his mom bolted upright with a hand on her chest. "Goodness gracious, Edward! You can't sneak up on me like that!"

He grinned. "Need help?"

"No, I have it, but thank you, honey."

Relief washed over him. He wanted to help but he hated laundry. It was pointless and so obnoxiously boring. Every week it was the same thing: Monday, wash the clothes and hang them to dry—even if they were worn for a day. Tuesday, wash the clothes and hang them to dry—even if they were worn for an hour. Wednesday, break day. Thursday, wash the clothes and hang them to dry—even if they were worn for a minute. Friday, Saturday, Sunday, same stuff. It was a vicious circle that never ceased to cycle around and around and around. Every. Dang. Day. *Almost.* His upper lip curled in disgust. Laundry was pointless, stupid, and dumb.

He watched as she pinned shirt after shirt. His eyes

rolled. How could she enjoy performing the monotonous motion of laundry this often? Repeating the same motion over and over. It was mind-numbingly dull and senseless. He huffed and folded his arms. His mom shot him a "*drop it*" look over her shoulder.

He shook his head. Never in his future was he going to *hang* laundry. Nope. Never. Honestly, neither should his mom. He knew doing laundry was written in the job description of being a mom, but doing it like this was medieval. People had washers and dryers now. Shoot, even his family had a washer. Why couldn't they also have a dryer?

Edward's eyes blazed. For the love of all that is holy, the neighbor lady down the road had a washer and a dryer, why don't they? The question tumbled over and over again in his mind. It didn't make any sense: she was a single woman with a lumbering job, she didn't have a husband because she had short hair, she wore baggy flannels, she had a faint moustache, and to top it all off, she had a nasty habit of chewing tobacco. How could a person, a woman like that, get a washer and a dryer, and they couldn't?

"I think we should get a dryer," he snapped as he strode to the house. He crossed his arms and turned his back to lean against the warm brick.

"Eddie," she warned, "I don't need this talk again. Your dad is on a peddle-run to Pennsylvania, and we don't have the…" Edward groaned loudly. She took a breath in. "I'm not havin' this discussion."

He didn't need to see his mother's face to know what it looked like right then. He knew her eyes were narrowed, her mouth was set and her cheeks were flushed. It was in her voice.

"Okay, so? We could just get one while he…"

"I can't lift a dryer on my own!" she barked, snapping a shirt to whip the wrinkles out from it, before pinning it up.

"Mom, you know I could…"

"You're too young. It'd break your back and…" She sighed. "Your daddy will be back next week, and then maybe we can talk about gettin' one."

He knew he should drop it but that didn't matter. What mattered was getting the dryer. Saving her hours of labor. Lessening the burden.

"That's too long from now! This…" he pressed on, pointing to the clothesline though she couldn't see him, "it's *so stupid, Mom!* You're out here for hours: in the cold, in the heat, and you don't want help! You just do it, like you're a slave!"

She turned sharply, shocked. "That is enough. You'll respect me and you'll respect your father. Now, go 'n play, before I get the mind to whip you for that kind of mouth."

Edward boiled. He hated this.

She sighed and slowly crossed her arms. "I know you care, honey, and I'm glad you do. I love you." She sighed and unfolded her arms, "We will get one soon enough. Now, go 'n play with your brother, and take a jacket, why don't you? It's gonna be gettin' a little chilly," she said, returning to her laundry.

"Fine. Love you, too."

He pushed off the wall and jockeyed his weight through the door. He stood still, letting his eyes adjust and listened for a moment, trying to hear where Luke was. He was too mad to yell for him and if he did, he knew Luke would take it personally. He always took it personally.

Edward walked down the hallway to the base of the stairs and leaned into its railing while he waited. Taking a deep breath, his mood soured even further. He spat on the carpet. The air in the house floated around him, its fermented stink making his nose twitch. Silty and stagnant, it smelled like the previous owners. Disgusting. They must've been smokers. He huffed, got to love perfumed cigarette dust and aged wood musk. Taking a deep breath, Edward tried to clear his mind.

Focusing on the negative wouldn't change the situation. Focus, focus, focus. The negatives were annoying, but he owed it to his mom and Luke to be in a good mood.

On his third exhale, a large whine and two thuds snapped his eyes to the ceiling. Luke was upstairs. Edward almost smacked his forehead. Duh, he must be getting the walking stick.

Bounding up the steps, taking two at a time, Edward took a sharp turn into his parents' doorway.

Luke had left it wide open. Smirking, he came to a stop and took in the image.

Luke had jammed his shoulder and head under the low-standing frame of their parents' queen-sized bed. Edward couldn't help but laugh. Luke looked as if he'd been half-swallowed.

"Giving up already?"

"I can't reach the st-stick! It's too f-far away..." Luke's response was muffled.

"Well no shit, Sherlock. Your arms are too short, like you. And your butt's too big to fit all the way under the bed. Move out of the way. Let a real man do the job," Edward barked his command and grabbed Luke's ankles, yanking to slide him backward.

Edward climbed onto his stomach, replacing Luke to give it a whirl.

"Hey!" Luke screeched. "I don't have a b-big butt..." Luke whined. "Mom says not to cuss."

"'M-mom said not to cuss'," Edward mocked in a girly voice.

"Don't m-mock me. I didn't stutter on *Mom.*"

Edward could almost see Luke's mouth twisted in a grimace and his arms crossed. He smiled to himself, can't let him have the whole day off without a little picking.

Edward saw the stick and knew he could reach it, though he was surprised Luke couldn't. He may have been fourteen, but Edward was only four inches taller than Luke.

Yeah, that made his arms two inches longer, but Edward was small for his age. Edward stuck out his tongue and reached further, Dad said he'd hit his growth spurt soon.

Extending his arm under the bed as much as he could, Edward reached for the stick. An aggravated huff puffed from his chest. Not quite. He dug his toes into the hard wood floor and jammed his shoulder into the frame. He walked his fingers across the seams of timber, clinging to every inch further he could get. The skin of his back, shoulder, and arm tingled as it stretched of his muscles.

Luke kicked at the bedframe. "What's taking so long?"

"Nothing." Edward sounded winded, "I almost have it."

"Well, hurry up!" Luke complained.

"Shut... Up..." Edward panted.

"Mom said not to s-say 'shut up'."

Edward's eyes rolled so hard they ached in his skull.

Why was he even helping Luke? He was so annoying. Sure, Luke could take his time, but God forbid Edward—

Edward's fingers brushed the hard, smoothed surface of the polished walking stick and he quickly flicked it into his palm. Army wiggling his body backwards and out from under the bed, he sat up on his knees and handed the stick to Luke.

"There," he puffed.

Luke smirked as he snatched it and stood it upright on the floor in front of his small body. Luke was all arms and legs. A stringbean of a boy.

Edward pursed his lips and cocked his head to the side. Luke was only a little taller than the stick now. Gee, what was it? Three, four inches taller? Five, max. Edward brushed back the hair from his forehead. Luke was growing so much…and too fast too. He wished in that moment their father was there. Dad didn't get to see anything anymore. He missed all the big moments. Edward's twelfth birthday. Lukes first time riding a bike. He was always gone on a run, hauling whatever they needed him to, to wherever they needed it to be.

Luke's eyes narrowed. "It's shorter; what'd you do to it?"

"Nothing," Edward said casually, "you just got taller."

Luke pulled the stick towards his chest and hugged it tightly. "Oh. Cool!"

"C'mon, don't break it," Edward warned. "It was pap-pap's."

Luke loosened his arms and his smile dropped. "Right,... so, are you ready?"

"Yeah, let's go." Edward stood up and wiped at his

jeans and shirt. Evidence of the stick scramble etched on them with dust. Gross.

With a small sigh and a scuff of his shoe on the ground, Luke looked up at Edward. "Eddie, what kind of gun should I make today?"

"Make it whatever you want. We're going."

Edward pushed past Luke down the stairs. As he reached the bottom, he gripped the ball of the railing and swung his body around. The momentum sent him flying onto the hallway's cool floor and headed for the backdoor. As he put his hand around the knob, he heard Luke's feet begin their trot down the stairs.

Edward's eyes closed tightly. Why was he so *slow*? Luke took forever to do anything, and Edward's biggest pet peeve was untimeliness. He hated waiting. It made the two of them together a bad combination.

Every single day, his little brother found something to take a lifetime to do. One time, Luke took forever to eat breakfast. He cut tiny pieces off his egg and place them in his mouth so slowly a sloth could climb a tree faster. Another time, Luke took forever to do his chores. Edward couldn't pawn off *any* of his onto him that day. Then today, Luke took forever to reach the stick. It made Edward's skin warm and his palms sweat. If something needed to get done, it should be done on time and in the right way. Wasted time is the worst crime.

Edward twisted the knob. The free air cleansed his lungs and he walked up the hill. He sat on the grass, and listened to the quiet. From a distance, he heard the faint "Aaaggh!" of the axe-swinging lady next door. She must adore chopping wood.

Edward shivered as he remembered meeting her for the very first time. He and his dad had gone over to ask if she needed help. She had been cawing and growling and howling all morning. If Edward had been her, he'd have been embarrassed. His brows furrowed as he remember setting eyes on her. She must have been six feet tall, and she was built like a... bear.

She had been in mid swing as they walked over the low fence. She had grunted, swung the axe back over her shoulder, and hollered until the sharpened edge pierced and split the wood.

The memory sent chills bubbling up his spine and caused the scrambled eggs of that morning's breakfast to stir uncomfortably. She was an animal, and though he'd never admit it, she intimidated him.

Luke was finally out of the house and up the stretch of green by the time the chills faded. "Ready?"

Edward smirked as he stood, "Yeah."

"Okay."

"Hey, where's your…"

Edward grabbed the nearest stick and jerked his knee up, breaking it in two. He waggled them at Luke.

"Pistols?"

"Mhm!" Edward fake shot Luke and he pretended to die, falling dramatically to the ground, clutching his heart.

"Ahh! No.. I'm… dying… Tell… my wife… I… blehhhhh!" Luke grinned with his tongue out as he faked his death. Edward laughed, helping Luke back to his feet.

"Come on, goon."

"Okay!" Luke clumsily stood to his feet and turned to look at their mom. "Bye, Momma! Love you!"

She looked up from the basket. "I love you too, baby! I love you, Eddie!" she said, raising the tone of her voice on his name and waving her arm.

Edward smiled and turned to look back. "Yeah, love you too."

They entered the woods and began the trek to the clearing they loved to use. Silence puddled around them as their strides synced together.

"You decide on what kind of gun that walking stick is going to be or what?" Edward asked.

"Uh, I think I want to make it a rifle."

"Luke, you always make it a rifle," he groaned.

Luke squinted. "*So*?"

"Okay. Whatever. You remember the rules?" Edward reached over and ruffled his hair.

"Yeah." Luke swatted at his arm.

"Okay, what are they?" Edward challenged.

"Remain unseen."

Edward put one finger out on his left hand. "Yep."

"Work together to kill the enemy."

A second finger up, "Yup."

"Stay quiet, stay close, and always…" Luke hesitated, "…Turn the safety on?"

"No? It's not a real gun, Luke." Edward said.

"But Dad said-"

"But Dad nothing," Edward snapped, his voice a little harsher than he intended. They came to a stop. Luke frowned and held up his walking stick. Placing the butt of the stick into his shoulder and pretending to aim, he shot at unseen enemies.

"All right. Who are we fighting?" Edward asked.

"Hmmmmmm." Luke tilted his face to the sky then spun to face Edward. "Let's fight the Brits!"

"Okay," Edward laughed, "it'd be cooler to fight Indians... but whatever you say small fry."

"Cool, let's talk strategy." Luke crouched in the leaves. They crunched softly and Edward mirrored his movements. Even though it was late summer, he loved how the forest floor always had leaves on it.

They spoke in hushed tones and the world about them transformed. Instantly, the woods began flourishing with greener, more youthful leaves. The usually faint perfume of the Appalachian Mountain mint evolved and grew stronger as they fell further into their imaginations. Their voices became that of the colonel and the sergeant.

For Edward, as the colonel, his voice became deeper and it rattled with the gravel of grown masculinity. For Luke, as the sergeant, his voice sunk, as low as he could get it, into to a lavish baritone. That of a kind, southern gentleman. Both voices were laden with the liquor of southern charm.

"Now, look 'ere. The Brits 'ave moved in from the northeast," Edward said as he brushed the leaves from the ground. Taking a twig, he outlined the 'known,' path of the British army. "It can be assum'd they've moved along this edge of the woods," he made a circle, "right 'ere. Now, if I'm correct, and Sergeant, I usually am, they will strike," he made an X, "'ere."

"Mhmm..." Luke's brows pinched together.

Edward continued, excitement bubbling up like freshly poured soda. "Yuh sees, if we comes up through this 'ere patch of pines," he pointed to the right, "and attack their flank, it'll go lot betta. Why Sergeant... we'd have the element of surprise!" Edward sat back on his heels, letting pride swell in his chest. He waited for Luke to applaud him.

A minute passed and still, the quizzical look sat on Luke's face. It was a good. The tactics were right, the Brits would be taken back by their attack. They'd win for sure. Why didn't Luke see that already?

A few more minutes passed. Edward got impatient. "Now, Sergeant, do you believe this to be the proper plan of attack?"

"Well, I say, Colonel..." Luke answered. "After some thinkin'... I think that is a mighty fine way... to die. Yuh sees, we are in the mountain country, sir, and it'd be betta if we mov'd tuh the left of that there camp... stay long the base of these 'ere mountains. We'll 'ave the dark of the brush behind us, makin' our uniforms blend inta the forest."

Luke made his own line in the dirt. Edward studied that line. He felt the depression of his swollen pride getting smaller and smaller. It stung to not be the brightest strategist seated in the leaves, but it felt better knowing his little brother was growing up. Getting wiser. Edward let out a sigh and in one sweeping motion, he wiped their plan off the dirt.

The colonel and sergeant agreed to the plan and back in the zone they submerged. It was crucial to never leave evidence behind for the enemy to see. Edward swept his hand across the clear view of their plan of attack, erasing it from view in one foul swoop. If the Brits found it, it would surely seal the deal for their defeat in battle.

"Let's move out!" Luke whisper-yelled and began

crawling towards his marked path.

"Wait!" Edward squeaked and stood up. He cleared his throat and coughed, he forgot to settle back into his baritone. In a more masculine pitch, "Look!"

Edward stepped closer to a pile of leaves, crouching back down from his stance. Pointing at it with one hand, he beckoned Luke back with the other. The leaves were haphazardly shaped, oddly lying there like the corpse of a fallen soldier. Ahhh… maybe it *was* a fallen soldier. Edward kicked at them and the leaves dispersed, revealing what he had already assumed: a British spy, dead from Nightlock!

"Dumb fella ate the berries. Caught the worst of it, I think. We mus' be close." Edward hissed, snarling his nose in disgust.

"Loot 'em," Luke suggested, "he might have somethin' useful."

When Edward rustled around the figure, he felt a hard rectangular shape. He pushed it and it gave, in that familiar way cardstock does.

Making eye contact with Luke, he shoved his hand into the Brit's pocket and plucked out a folded letter. Edward read it out loud. Every word made both boys clench their jaws and grit their teeth.

"Those filthy mongrels!" Luke scuffed the ground with the ball of his foot.

"The level of deceit goes beyond! It's not a league of soldiers we are huntin' after all," Edward rued quietly, his words almost inaudible. "No. Rather, a well-oiled squadron of highly skilled mercenaries… Oh, how I hate the English!" Edward crumpled his letter and tossed it to the ground.

Mercenaries were bad enough on their own, as one singular individual. They were hauntingly worse as a group. They would be nearly impossible to beat. Edward shook his head and Luke spit at the ground. This was going to be harder than imagined. Each of these individuals was a master of finding the unfindable and of killing the unkillable.

It was up to them, the colonel and the sergeant, to take them out and save the revolution, but would the plan still work? Should they re-strategize or should they trust Sergeant's plan and move forward?

"What should we do, Colonel?" Luke's voice broke the silences swirling through the trees.

Edward tucked the letter into the sleeve of his jacket and wiped his hands on his pants. "We continue with the plan, Sergeant, and if we get inta trouble, well, we handle it."

Luke smiled and nodded.

Edward and Luke maneuvered intricately along their established line. They swiveled their heads back and forth, eyeballing each tree, each leaf, each bush and twig, closely, cautiously. They searched painfully for the Special Operations Unit, but only more forest opened before them.

They pressed forward, combing through the woods, over rocks, under fallen tree trunks, and across a creek. Edward noted that their patriot gear blended nicely into the pine, just as Luke had said. They wouldn't be spotted even if—

Suddenly, a branch snapped and the leaves crunched. Edward shot a tightly clenched fist into the air. Luke stopped immediately at his signal and crouched down. He watched his brother closely, and their ears strained to hear it once more.

Whistles of birds transformed. They became the chitter-chatter of hushed voices over a crackling fire. Barking squirrels became the faint laughter floating from a camp. The clunk of the woodpecker's trill became the clanking of musket bags being tossed to rest against the bases of trees. They thought they were alone... oh how wrong they were. Edward turned his head towards Luke and signaled a flanked maneuver. Luke nodded.

Edward had only taken his first step to the left when the hairs on his neck stood and the revolutionary world faltered before him and fizzled out. A loud, guttural wail rippled noisily through the tops of the trees. Luke froze. Edward could feel his little brother's eyes on him. When he turned his head to reassure Luke it was okay, the same squeal of a scream broke into the silence again. What is that noise? It didn't sound like any animal he had heard before. The emotion wriggling within it was unrecognizable... Was it in pain? Was it hunting? Was it hurt?

His stomach sank and flipped uneasily as a third, more strained and almost woman-sounding wail tore through them once more.

The sound electrifying in the worst way possible. Its sharp and uncomfortable pitch pierced him, making his blood run ice cold. His hands trembled as he studied Luke's small frame. His brother looked pale, scared. The air shifted. The fading warmth of the sub blocked out by the fear sinking its claws around them. That call, that kind of sound, made your skin crawl and your mouth dry. Edward took a deep breath in, and held it.

Seconds passed too slowly as he waited for it to erupt once more. For the cry to run ripples of shock down his spine.

Seconds turned to minutes, and Edward's statued figure, loosened. The coast felt clear. As the ease of the passing time warmed him further, he slowly and painfully released the air.

What could that have been? What made a sound like that? Edward racked his brain, filtered through his memories, and dug up the one explanation that could make the most sense. Loud. Obnoxious. Womanly.

It was too obvious. How had he missed this?

His mind slowed his heart: the neighbor. It had to be the lady next door… Well, a lady *of sorts*. She was sort of manly…

"Luke," Edward laughed, duck-walking to close the distance between them, "it's just the neighbor."

"But that…" The stick quivered in Luke's hand.

"No, no. Seriously, I'm sure of it. It has to be her. We are probably pretty close to the field she chops wood in. You know how she is!" Edward mocked swinging an axe and screaming loudly. Luke grinned at his performance.

Edward beat his chest and flexed his muscles. "I am woman! Graaaaaah! I chop wood! Graaaah! I need no man!"

"Y-you s-sound…" Luke stuttered through his laugher," j-j-just like… her! Haha! She is so loud!"

"I *know* she is, but I mean, I would be too if I had no friends and nothing better to do," Edward said, nonchalantly.

Waving them forward, Edward let the world slip into

the past once more. "Come on, Sergeant. Let's get back to the mission."

Luke nodded and his face fell serious. "I can 'ear the men ov'r there, sir, but we need visuals."

Edward pointed to the top of a nearby hill. It looked a little unfamiliar, and for a moment, panic pulled him from the game. He shrugged it off. They probably walked a little further than what they were used to, but he could get them back, no problem.

"If we reach the top of that there hill's crest, we will 'ave a better look at how their camp is set up—then we can continue with our attack and ambush those S.O.U.s. You 'ave your rifle loaded, Sergeant?"

Luke lifted his rifle and opened its chamber. He turned his head sideways and squinted down the barrel.

"Yes'sir," he concluded.

"Good. You move up tuh the east this time, Sergeant, and I'll take the west."

The sun, unnoticed by Edward, was setting fast, making the colors of the evening a fine mixture of painted amber rays. As Edward and Luke reached the top, Edward righted himself into a kneeling position.

Shoving the barrels of his small pistols into the sides of his jeans, Edward peered over the hill's edge.

As the forest poured out before him, they envisioned the S.O.U.'s camp once more.

Out of the bushes and stumps formed the crew's baggage, their disheveled sleeping quarters, and the gear of each mercenary. It was easy to see they were weary from their long journey to find the rebels. A broken tree, cinched at its half and tilted forward over the ground became a large tent. Edward already knew it was filled with the belongings of the leader: Telman.

That was the one Edward wanted, and he was going to get him. Telman showed his face in every game. He was the baddest of men, and not in the cool way. He routinely performed atrocities that Edward hated. Luke and Edward had seen first hand the lengths of evil that wrapped like vines around Telman's black heart. Edward's stomach churned at the memory of seeing Telman posing as the Indian Chief, scalping a young child he had ripped from the colony woman's arms.

Both boys sucked in their breath, and released it raggedly. The camp before them was magnificent.

Edward was the first to speak, "I see Telman's quarters... do you have a visual of the troops?"

Luke squinted hard. "Mm-hm, yep, I sure do, Colonel. There are two that I can see, but there may be more in that there tent over yonder. One of them looks tuh be sittin' on their gear, and," Luke chuckled, "one is peein' by that there tree. Do you see 'em?"

"Haha! What idiots! I see 'em. They ain't got no clue. Okay. I'm goin' tuh move 'round tuh the west and take out who's in the tent. Hopefully, that's where Telman is hidin' too. If not, I'll find him..." Edward gritted his teeth and pointed down the hill to the soldiers in plain sight. "I need you to get the man on the gear and the one pissin'."

"Yes'sir." Luke began to crawl, then stopped and looked back to Edward. "Do you think they'll run after the first shots blow?"

Edward gave a toothy grin, "I sure hope so. I love a good chase."

As Edward duck-walked to his post at the peak of the eastern hill, he decided to descend towards the tent. Luke wouldn't care. He knew Luke would be sprawled out in the leaves, lying on his belly, aimed and waiting for the right moment. Locked in his own zone, preparing to peg those Brits.

Or at least, he hoped.

Clenching his jaw against the trumpet protest of leaves, he wished suddenly that the weather wasn't slipping into autumn. That it was still mid-summer and his footfalls were still blanketed by more youthful leaves rather than these loud and obnoxious ones.

The burning in his thighs amplified with each step closer. His heart pounded in his chest, anxiety blooming ember-like heat behind his ears. Or was it excitement? Edward shrugged; same thing, different names.

When he reached the back of the tent, he took a deep breath. He turned to scan the foliage and find Luke. Edward needed to make eye contact one last time with the sergeant before he'd give signal to unleash fury. When the boys' eyes zeroed in on one another, Edward lifted his right hand, pointed two fingers up, and pressed them forward.

In an instant, Edward hurled his body from the crouch he was in. Like a sprinter exploding from block, he exploded through the white cotton of the tent. Unsheathing each pistol from his side pockets, he knocked back the hammers and fashioned a smirk on his face.

"Mornin' fellas," he said, his southern accent thickened in the excitement. Two startled British mercenaries turned at him, but Edward was too fast.

"Pow! Pow!" He shot them, popping two bullets into

each of their chests.

Edward had deadly aim. The men clutched helpless at the blossoming dark red blooms on their chest before their bodies fell, smacking the dirt with satisfying thuds. Pride tugged at the corners of his mouth, turning his smug smile into a genuine grin. They never saw it coming. Everything was going according to plan.

Adrenaline rippled around him, filling his muscles with newfound energy and joy. It heated his body. Even so, the battle was not over yet. He needed to find Telman. His eyes scanned painfully over the tent. His heart raced even quicker as he heard the bang from Luke's rifle fire twice.

"Bang! Bang!"

Aw, yeah! There is no doubt the boys got them this time. Edward beamed behind his hunter's gaze. Luke had been spot on. An ambush was the perfect plan: unknown, unprepared for, unsuccessfully fought against. A soft chuckle silently fell from his lips. The men are down, the only thing left to do was find Telman.

Edward placed his pistols under his arm and pulled his shirt up to wipe the sweat falling from his chin. As the cool air replaced the place of his t-shirt, he grew more suspicious. Where is Telman? He's too clumsy to be this good at hiding. Yes, he was evil and sinister and the reincarnation of Satan himself, but he was not sneaky. Telman was not smart.

Edward shook his head rapidly. He couldn't have gotten far, his camp was here.

Edward's head swiveled and landed on Luke's approaching figure. For a moment, he forgot Telman. He was proud of his brother. Truly, he couldn't stop applauding the plan utilized.

Even in execution of the strategy, Luke's skill had improved. Luke had waited *just* long enough to hear Edward's pistols fire before taking his own shots. He had known that Edward's shot would provide the right amount of stunned surprise to get the men thrown off. It made them easy targets. Luke had never thought so far-forward in battle before now.

Edward's mind wandered to his father. He has learned this rule while hunting with him. Similar rules applied when deer hunting, especially from the ground. When those thin, twiny legs carried that deer into the line of sight, it was pertinent that you wait. When the deer finally place its body just so, giving the hunter a shot, the hunter needed to bleat at it. The bleat mimicked a fawn, and the deer, confused, stopped. Leaving itself in a perfect shot zone, and standing still. Next thing the deer knows: Bang! It's dead, just like these red-coat good-for-nothings.

Luke had just closed the distance when the loud crashing of leaves snapped Edward back into the game. Telman. A little ways beyond the tent, the boys watched as Telman took off running, his escape filling the silence with the *'ka-crash'* of footsteps.

Edward bolted from the tent, pushing his legs into an Olympic sprint. He could see the back of the general's heading back toward the creek.

"We have to catch him!" Luke yelled, his voice echoing between the trees.

"Easy!" Edward called over his shoulder.

Edward and Luke ran, blurring their images in the forest. Anyone who saw them would see only a smudgy essence of them. Their lungs burned and their legs ached for relief, for oxygen, but they pressed forward. The mission wasn't over.

"Let's go!" Edward grunted, pushing himself harder, pulling further away from Luke.

The red coat of Telman's jacket was disappearing with each passing second and he wasn't about to let him get away. No way. Not now. This was important; this was life or death for him, his brother, and his country. Edward grimaced. He begged his legs to move faster.

Why was Telman so fast?

As the jacket faded into nothing, Edward slowed down. He wanted to cuss. He wanted to cry. This couldn't be it? This can't be the end? How could Telman get away... No. This isn't right... They needed to win. He grabbed his hair and massaged his scalp. How could he let him get away? He stopped walking.

A soft whistle caught his attention. Edward looked back at Luke, but Luke wasn't looking at him. He was looking past him and pointing. Edward traced the direction and scanned the woods. He let out a sigh. Not even twenty yards in front of him, Telman's elbow peeked out from behind a tree. The sleeve of his red coat flickered and twitched in the wind. The boys regrouped, analyzed a plan and circled to either side of the tree. Another ambush.

Luke and Edward drug their feet as slowly and quietly as they could. When they were close enough, each of them raised their weapons.

"Boom!"

"Bam!"

"Yea-esss!" Edward wailed, dropping one of his pistols

and thrusting a clenched fist into the air. "We got him!"

"Wooooo-hoooo!" Luke hollered, "We won!"

Edward closed the distance between them and wrapped his sweaty arms around the shoulders of his younger brother. "Good job, buddy. You saved the revolution!"

"T-thanks, Eddie!" Luke said into Edward's chest, laughing. As Edward pulled away from his brother, he dropped the other stick to the ground. It had lost its guise of imagination.

"That was fun," Luke said. Edward nodded. "Do you think we could p-play again?"

"No, not today. We have to head back. It's getting pretty dark and," Edward rubbed his stomach, "I'm hungry."

Luke's stomach growled at Edward's mention of food, and he agreed to start heading back. As they walked, Luke began to chatter off and on about the mission. He was proud of himself, and Edward couldn't blame him. He had outdone himself. In Edward's mind, Luke had moved up in rank because of this performance today. Though, he'd never let Luke know it.

They walked in the fading light. The sun was setting behind the ridge as their feet passed over the forest floor. It had been a good day. The sky had been clear, the weather a happy medium between cool and warm. They had even successfully defeated the S.O.U. of British mercenaries. Now they were heading home for dinner. Luke grabbed a pinecone from the ground and threw it at Edward.

Edward smiled and punched his arm. He felt good, but a small uncertainty boiled at the pit of his stomach. The sun sank lower beneath the horizon, leaving the smallest of its beams peaking over the edge. Why weren't they home yet?

He glanced around, scratching briefly at the back of his neck. Something felt off. The trees looked unfamiliar, and they had yet to pass the patch of brush that smelled of sweet mountain mint.

Minutes floated by like hours. Edward felt nerves bubbling up his throat as he side-stared at his little brother. A twinge of guilt twisted him as he heard Luke's stomach growl.

The last of the cool, pale yellow beams vanished and Edward knew they still were nowhere near home. At least, not to his knowledge. Nothing around them gave sign of being near home.

In the distance, the wails began to cry out once more. Louder than they had been earlier—that was a good sign! A bit of relief trickled over Edward. Maybe they were getting close after all.

Edward shook his hands and breathed into his palms before rubbing them together. He couldn't believe this lady was still out there. It was dusk and the temperature was dropping. He was sure she had enough fire wood to last winter after today, what more could she need? He glanced at Luke and Luke's expression asked the same question: How could one person still be chopping wood?

Edward sighed heavily and grinned at Luke. "She's still going at it!"

"Haha! What a w-weirdo!" Luke agreed.

The boys laughed together, listening to the sound in the distance. Yelping, yowling, yodeling... every five or ten minutes.

"I bet Mom's worried," Edward said, somewhat joking, somewhat concerned.

"Yeah, she worries a lot…"

"She'll be fine, though. We should almost be there!"

"Think she made rolls?"

"I hope so."

They looked forward and squinted into the blackening forest, searching for breaks in the trees before them. The uneasy feeling stirred again, somehow more coldly, at the bottom of Edward's stomach. The feeling reminded him he wasn't all that sure they weren't lost.

Had he set a small Bridger of his own, ambushing them into a sprung trap of the woods around them? He could hear his mother now: *I can't believe you got lost! I told you to be careful! You're grounded!*

He felt Luke's hand press into his. His first instinct was to pull away, but he fought it. It felt nice in the cold, and the warmth settled the storm raging inside. Edward knew he had to get them home. He had to get them out of the night and into the warmth of their house.

Or anywhere away from the shifting figures of the night. Shivers raced down his spine. He hated it.

The forest had begun to take on a life of its own, breathing with new sounds, moving with unseen creatures.

"What was that?" Luke whispered, pointing into the night. He squeezed Edward's hand.

Edward squinted but couldn't see what he was pointing at. "I don't see anything; what does it look like?"

"I think it's a deer… like… bedded down," Luke whispered.

"Let's get closer."

"No!" Luke squealed. "What if it wakes up?"

"So what if it does? It's just a deer, Luke. Plus, we'll be quiet, okay?"

"Okay…"

They both moved closer. Each boy took extra care to not make any more noise than they had to. As they neared the figure, Edward perked up, finally seeing the form Luke was talking about.

"Hey!" he whispered, "I see it."

"Shhhh!" Luke hissed.

The boys paused as a stench filled the air. Oh god, it was awful. Edward swatted at the air, but the smell didn't dissipate; it permeated. Ugh, it was a smell that could singe hundreds of nose hairs with each unwelcomed inhale. Like old sweaty socks that had been drenched in vomit and left in the sun to bake, it clung to the air before them. It pressed against their faces, a mask of the worst kind of musk.

Every breath was painfully disgusting. Edward felt his breakfast churn and climb his throat. He swallowed hard, forcing it back down.

Tiny, floating gnats began bouncing off their faces, growing thicker as they took one step closer. Now only five feet away, Luke had been right. It was a deer, but it sure wasn't bedded down. It was dead.

Like D.E.A.D., dead.

Long gone dead.

Half-decayed dead.

Don't go near it if you don't want to lose your lunch kind of dead.

Edward's breakfast of eggs tossed nauseously in the catacombs of his stomach, threatening to make an appearance for the second time that day.

As the boys moved even closer, Edward realized, it didn't only smell horrid, it looked horrid.

The body of the deer had been shredded. The throat had been ripped out and the innards were strewn backwards. Gnats and flies were dancing across the bloodied flesh but preferred the eyes of the deer that were left open, cakey, and void of life.

"What do you think got it?"

Edward jumped, startled by Luke's voice. "Uh... I don't know... maybe a bear? I know there are plenty out this way."

Timidly, Luke reached out to touch it. "Don't touch it!" Edward yelled.

"Why?"

"Because it cou..."

A long, drawn-out growl reverberated from behind the deer. They both froze. ""What..." Luke swallowed, "what, was that?"

Edward opened his mouth to answer but only silence slipped out. His heart began beating violently, flooding his ears with a rhythm close to an off-balanced washer. As another growl seeped across the blood-matted belly of the deer, Edward grabbed hold of Luke's shoulder. The hairs on his neck stood. This growl was lower, more menacing.

"Don't. Move."

That was a good rule of thumb. Don't move, stay still. They won't attack if you don't move. Edward held his breath. His dad had said, *when an animal is ready to attack, it typically won't move until you move.*

"What is it?" Luke whispered back. He stood stock-still.

Edward couldn't answer. He didn't know how to answer. He couldn't see it. Images of creatures that made those noises streamed through his mind. It couldn't be a bear. Bears don't rip throats out and they eat from the belly. It couldn't be a wolf or coyote either. Wolves weren't local and coyotes moved in packs. If it were a coyote, there would be more than one growling at them.

Edward shivered. He could only picture it as some monstrous *thing* behind the shredded, torn deer. Some hideous *thing* cloaked in darkness before them. A *thing* with soulless eyes and long, yellow teeth that were filled with rotting flesh. A *thing* with wiry, patched fur that left exposed, wrinkled pockets of skin.

He pushed the image away. Another low growl cut through his thoughts, startling them both. As the growl hilted into a high-pitched hiss, Edward knew what it was.

The yowl was crisp and piercing to their eardrums.

It was a mountain lion.

The day came rushing back to him. The man-lady yelling, her howling—that wasn't *her*.

It was this thing before them! This… cat was now crawling closer and closer.

Heat flushed through his frame, and he knew right then that he had to get Luke out of there! Edward shook his head, hands clambering around to find Luke behind him. Those calls… How foolish could he have been? No one yells while cutting wood. He should've known those calls. He should've gotten them back sooner. He should've remembered. His father had said, *female mountain lions scream when in heat.*

How could he forget? How could he have jeopardized so much? Himself! Luke! Shaking, he knew what he had to do. He had to get Luke out of here; this wasn't a game anymore.

Suddenly, he felt tugged forward as his body hilted over. Edward watched in horror as his little brother fell into the leaves before him. Edward waved his arms hoping to stop himself from toppling over on top of him. Immediately, Luke began apologizing but Edward couldn't hear him. All Edward cared about was pulling him up from the ground. All Edward heard was the shifting of leaves under paws and the screech of the forest cat before him.

"Luke, hey." Edward's voice shook, shuddering with each word. He closed his fists around Luke's shirt and yanked him to his feet. Spinning him around, the words poured quickly from his mouth. "Luke, look at me! Hey, hey. Look at me." Luke's wide eyes settled onto Edward's face. "Let's play another game" Luke shook his head and Edward's heart fell as he saw tear pooling in his little brother's eyes. "C'mon. Let's play one last game tonight, yeah? I'm going to stay here and count to three."

"W-what i-i-is t-that, Eddie?" The words were caught in Luke's throat, causing him to stutter more than usual.

"Oh, that? Pffft, it's nothing! Just a big ole' bobcat... Yeah, a bobcat. That's it! It's," he waved his hand, "harmless!"

"O-oh... okay," Luke whimpered.

"Right, okay. So this time, we're going to play a racing game."

Another hiss filled the air, and more leaves crunched. Edward felt time slipping like sand in an hourglass. He was running out of time to get Luke out of there.

"I don't w-want to p-p-play a racing g-game." Luke grabbed his hand. "I'm scared!"

Edward was too. He pictured the big cat again. Its face distorted in a snarl. Its tan fur, hidden by the ink of night, tattered and rough. Its yellow eyes glowing under the invisible blue hue of the moon. Its mouth hanging open, hot breath panting, with teeth ready to… *No*. Focus.

"You have to, okay?" He grabbed Luke's face, wiping the tears before slowly turning him toward what he hoped would be the best path home. "I want you to run as fast as you can… as fast as your legs will carry you. You *have* to beat me. You have to make it back home *first*." Luke let out a soft whimper and nodded his head. "You can do this. It'll be fun!" Edward patted his shoulder. "I'll be right behind you."

Terror settled into Edward's bones then, causing his hands to tremble. He squeezed Luke's shoulders tightly, hoping to stop them. Hoping Luke hadn't noticed.

"Straighten up. I'm not taking no for an answer, yuh hear me, Sergeant? This is an order from yur colonel, understood?"

Edward felt Luke's shoulders stiffen under his hands, "Sir, yes, sir."

"On the count of three."

Edward's voice shook more violently now. The pressure of holding onto Luke's shoulders released any control he thought he had in taming the shakes. The images of the mountain lions repeated in his mind, no matter how many times he tried to blink them away. It must be stacked… a hefty three feet off the ground and weigh anywhere from a hundred and forty to two hundred and twenty pounds.

Cold beads of sweat brimmed on his brow, forming only to chill him further, refusing to stream down his body. Cotton filled his mouth as a tightness gripped his chest. It squeezed any remaining air from his lungs. Edward shook more violently. He's dead. D.E.A.D., dead.

Edward took a steadying breath. "One."

Luke could make it home. "Two."

Luke had a chance to live. "Three."

Edward shoved Luke forward and yelled at the top of his lungs, "RUN!"

At the same moment he felt the soft fabric of Luke's jacket leave his fingertips, Edward faltered under the weighted pressure of heavy paws on his back. The large, sharpened claws rip through his t-shirt and sank into his flesh. He felt the slicing of his muscles, his nerves, his tendons. The sting was incomparable to anything he'd ever felt before.

"Eddie!" Luke's voice called. No!

"Go!" he yelled, straining against the pain. Hard teeth sank into his scalp, grinding against the hard surface of his skull. The loud sound sent shivers through his pinned body and his eye seared, released hot water down his cheek.

The lion pulled back to strike once more. Its exposed claws caught the side of his face and propelled him onto his back. Warm liquid run down his neck. He felt sick from the burning sensation pounding from all around him. He felt heavy and way too warm. All of his clothes damp against him.

Blow after blow landed, the lion's jaw unsure of where

they could get the best grip. His arms fought to find its neck but he was weak. The lion lifted and crashed onto his chest, pinning him further into the ground. Edward heard the snapping of his ribs before he felt their sharp, unmistakable breaks. The crippling anguish compounded into a blistering swelter that consumed his torso. He let out a wild cry. Somehow, that made his wounds feel a little better.

Edward screamed again with what little air he had in his lungs, hoping it'd relieve more of the hell he found himself in. He almost laughed at how pathetic it came out. It pooled and puddled around him, like the warmth leaving his body. Hope glimmered and swam away; he felt lighter from it... Maybe giving in to the black pool was good... it felt weightless and welcoming...

No, don't give in. Fight! Luke needs you! Think, Edward. Think!

That's when the light went off. In a moment of clarity, as paws continued grappling around his chest, he remembered. The light-headedness dropped from around him, and what his dad had told him about noise and mountain lions struck in the forefront of his mind. The right kind of noise could scare them... It needed to be high-pitched, loud... primal, like a bigger predator.

How? His last scream had been so weak. He shook his head only a little as the hot breath of the lion pelted against his face. He looked up and met eyes with this creature. Suddenly he knew, this was the ultimate battle. This was not the S.O.U. This was real life-or-death. Not a scenario. No more games, no more make-believe, no more fake actions. He could be a real soldier. A real fighter.

The mountain lion stared down at him, menacingly

shrugging its upper lip over its teeth, rattling its tongue with the movement of its growl.

As it opened its jaws and crashed its teeth into his shoulder, the same fear of failure filled his mind like gray smoke. The doubt of their escape looming more and more clear. Using the torturous pain that bubbled up through his adrenaline, Edward sucked in another breath. The jaws of the lion clenched harder; he felt the snap of his collarbone. Good, he could use that as fuel.

Three.

Two.

One.

On his exhale, Edward screamed at the lion. A loud, anguish-driven guttural yell that tore at the back of his throat. He could feel it diminish his vocal cords. Through his pain he smiled.

The lion's jaws tightened.

Luke bounded through the woods, hearing behind him the unmistakable sound of his brother's scream; it was unnaturally twinged and too high for a fourteen-year-old. The scream sent him flying faster. If Edward had any chance of living, he'd have to get Dad's gun. He breached the tree line, felt hope swell in his chest as he saw the backdoor's light. He could save him. He just knew he could.

He could run in, get the rifle from the fireplace, and-

His mom burst through the door and ran to him, clasping him in a vice-like hug. "Oh, I'm so happy you're safe!" She cooed.

"M-m-mom!" He squirmed violently against her hold.

"I was worried to death! Where have you boys been?" she continued, holding him tighter.

"MOMMA!" Luke yelled.

She stopped and looked at him. Stunned. "Where's Eddie?"

"I need Dad's gun."

Her face faltered, "You, you what?" A smile played at the corners of her mouth, disbelief at the question toying at them.

Luke pushed past her and swung open the backdoor.

"Luke!" His mother called after him, but his ears didn't hear her, they couldn't hear her. All they heard was the piercing siren of Eddie's scream.

Luke's small hands quickly found their place around the body of the shotgun. With a deep breath, he pulled it from its resting place on the mantle. Soldiers, he thought, for real this time.

As he turned back towards the door, he found himself toe to toe with his mother. Her face was a quilt of worry, confusion, pain, and doubt. "Luke, honey. You can't be takin' that gun out in the woods. It ain't no bigger than you, baby. What do ya need it— Where is Eddie?"

His chest burned as his ears reddened. He didn't have time to explain, each second that passed meant more damage or worse to Eddie. He had to get back. Cool sweat dampened the fire burning within him, but it was no relief.

"I h-have to g-g-go, Momma. I have to s-save him."

Her voice caught in a choke. "Save Eddie? Honey, what is going on? You need to save Eddie? Where is he? What is going on?"

Luke darted around her skirt and bounded out of the backdoor. Pummeling into the ebony night, he stretched his legs through the shadows. Where was he? He had to be this way... right? That tree looked familiar, right? I've been here.

Panic wrestled with his stomach, sending its spiked vines spiraling up his throat. They stayed there and coiled. His breath became short and labored.

Edward would know what to do; he always knew what to do. Luke remembered the first time he had broken his arm. Eddie was there. He'd taken his flannel off and made a sling for Luke, gingerly placing it over his head and carefully tucking his arm into the wrap.

"You'll be all right, Luke. Everything will be fine." He had smiled down at Luke, and Luke had felt for the first time that Edward really cared. His eyes had held something other than annoyance—they held love.

Luke's heart seized up, gripped with pain. "Eddie!" he screamed. "Eddie, where are you?"

His voice rattled the emptiness of the forest, waking anything resting in the cloak of the dark. His feet stumbled over the leaves and branches on the ground, each one crackling and crunching under his weight. He pleaded with his eyes to penetrate the black surrounding him, but they refused. The woods around him remained a maze unknown.

He started running again, screaming over and over for Eddie. Praying, because that's what adults did when they got scared, to the big man upstairs that he would lead him towards his brother. The gun, with every step, grew heavier and heavier. His sweat-laden palms struggled to keep it in their grip. His breathing became shorter and shorter, and a wheezing sound, one he'd never heard before, began appearing at the top of each breath.

He could feel the wheeze more and more, the gooey, stringy feeling thickening as he ran. "Eddie!" Luke yelled, ripping the raw at the back of his throat even more. As he swallowed, he tasted blood.

Luke's legs began to waver, the muscles burning and singing at the nerves.

He slowed to a stop and dropped to his knees, the crash loud and obnoxious in the silence. Sobs began to wrack his body, shaking his tiny frame and making him cough up the wheezy goo from his run. "Eddie…" Luke whimpered.

Hot tears pooled and fell over his eyelids, racing down his cheeks and splashing into the dead earth below. It was his fault. Eddie was dead because of him. If they hadn't gone to play soldier today, Eddie would be fine. He'd be home, with Momma. He'd be sitting on the ground, reading his book and pretending that the world didn't exist.

Luke wiped hastily at the tears, swatting them away. Soldiers don't cry. Soldiers don't cry.

Soldiers.

Don't.

Cry.

He stood up then and readjusted the shotgun in his hands. He would find Eddie. He'd bring him home. He'd make this okay.

"We got a special mission, Sergeant Luke," he said to himself, squaring his shoulders and deepening his voice. "The Colonel's been captured. He might be bein' tortured." He sniffled and took his first step forward. "He may not be able to hear us, but I do know that that Colonel is a tough one. He'll hold out. We just have to find him. Stay safe, Sergeant. Don't ya get caught, too."

Luke steadied the gun and ran forward, feeling his new confidence dry the wetness in his eyes and alleviate the burning in his chest.

He had not gone five yards before his foot caught and slammed him to the ground. Twigs and leaves assaulted his face as his head smacked the surface of the forest and he felt sick from where the harsh metal of the barrel had slapped against his ribs. Ringing pinged in his ear from where his head had slammed into the not yet thawed earth.

"Aagghhh."

Luke froze. His muscles tightened as adrenaline pumped through his body.

"Eddie?" he whisper-yelled. Seconds passed too slowly as he waited, collecting like molasses puddling from a tree in mid-January.

Placing his hands beneath his shoulder, he pushed up from the ground, tucking his feet under his body. When he did this, another groan peeled across the vacant air. Luke's hands began pawing at the ground, searching and sifting. Before he knew it, he had found Eddie's leg. Thank God! He crawled towards Eddie, his hands trailing his brother's body. The back, the shoulders... the... head.

Luke hadn't felt the warmth collecting on his hands, and he had ignored the smell of rust and iron hanging onto the breeze. He shook Eddie's shoulders. "Eddie, Eddie! Wake up. I'm here, E-Eddie, you have to w-wake up. I b-brought Dad's gun. I-I'll kill it, Ed. I p-promise."

"L... Luke?" Eddie's voice was weak and drunk sounding. "Luke, you're safe...?"

His voice faded out as Luke's hands turned Edward over. He was heavy, unusually heavy. Luke grunted and dug the toes of his boots into the mud, using as much of his small frame as he could to get Eddie on his back.

Luke's breath caught in his lungs as Eddie's body finally fell onto its back. His breathing was shallow but even, that unfamiliar wheezing peaking each inhale. He looked at Eddie's face.

Oh, God... His face, or what used to be his face, was smeared black with blood. The skin around his right eye was marred and shredded. With shaking hands, Luke placed his palms on Eddie's chest, searching for any more wounds. He wasn't sure if that was what was supposed to be done, but he had seen nurses at the doctor's office do it.

Finally, the stench of blood flooded his nose, making his throbbing head ache with more virility. Luke's stomach churned and quivered. He choked back bile as his hands searched still for more wounds. He found them all right. Deep slashes made ridges of Eddie's chest.

Accidentally, Luke's finger slipped into the cavity of one and Eddie shrieked with pain. How was he going to get him out of here? How was he going to get him home? He was smaller than Eddie, weaker than Eddie. Tears welled in his eyes and his already shallow breathing became quicker. No. No, this wasn't real. This was a dream, a nightmare. Dad had told him about nightmares, how sometimes they feel real. Sometimes they sound, feel, and smell real, but you wake up. You always wake up and everything is okay. Everything is fine.

"You're going to be fine." Edward's voice played over and over in his mind. He could see Eddie's eyes from that day, radiating down on him. The love, the trust. Wake up, he thought, wake up Luke. It's a dream. A dream.

As the sobs settled back in, Luke screamed. It tore at his throat, and blood he had tasted earlier peppered over his tongue once more. Hysteria had begun to settle in, aggravating his pounding head. This was it. This was the end... Luke stood up suddenly, swaying unsteadily.

The night, still black, blurred. No. This wasn't fair. This wasn't a game! He sucked in air and screamed. Over and over and over.

"Luke..." Eddie whispered. Hearing his brother's voice snapped him out of his trance and he knelt back down. "Luke..."

"Eddie? Eddie, what is it?" His voice was shaking.

"Tell... Momma I'm s-sorry."

"Aw, Eddie. You ain't got nothin' to be sorry for," Luke said.

"I-I'm s-sorry."

He stroked Eddie's face and rested his head on his shoulder, closing his eyes. "You ain't got nothin' to be sorry for, Colonel."

They stayed there, still, together.

Luke's eyes began glowing pink and he thought he heard yelling, or was it chirping? He gently shook his head, wincing at the ever-persistent throb. How hard had he smacked the ground? The sun couldn't be up already. How long had they been there? A couple of hours? He could still feel the low and slow rise and fall of Eddie's chest.

He remembered then that Momma said sometimes people go away, when they're hurt like Eddie. That their time on the earth is done, and that big man people pray to takes them away.

Takes them to a place called home, or sometimes Heaven.

The rustling of leaves came from a distance. Luke's eyes shot open, and he glanced around for the shotgun. It was barely dawn and too dark for the sun to be up. Seeing it a few feet away, still lying where he had fallen, he scrambled. If that thing, that big bobcat or mountain lion had come back, he'd kill it. He'd only been taught once how to shoot, but he knew the basics. Put the butt of the gun in your shoulder, lay your cheek on the butt, use one eye to aim, and keep a steady finger on the trigger, not pulling, but ready for the shot when it comes. He'd kill it.

The rustling grew louder, almost as if multiples were coming. Did bobcats or mountain lions travel in packs? He sniffled and coughed. His head objected; it still ached from his fall over Eddie but that didn't matter. He blinked hard and felt the electricity livening up his body. He'd be ready. Soldier round three was here, and he'd be ready.

"Edward?"

"Luke!"

Wait, those weren't chirps. Those were *voices*. He threw down the gun.

"Over here!" he yelled, the sound of his voice cracked and rusty. "Hey! Over here! We're over here!"

"I hear someone! Luke? Eddie?"

The crashing grew louder and quicker. The strobe of flashlights bloomed largely in the distance. Their voices gained volume too. There was a voice among them that sent chills down his spine. A soft, familiar voice. A warm and calming voice.

Momma.

Within minutes, a flock of adults descended, and Luke's mother's arms wrapped securely around his body. He knew from her expression she had seen Eddie. He saw the horror and fear cloud over her face moments before being wrapped in her safety. The men, who had been carrying a blue quilted blanket, set it down and tenderly moved Eddie from the forest floor to its middle.

"Momma, I t-tried to… He was…" Luke's voice gave out as fresh tears pelted down his cheeks. She pushed him back and looked dead into his eyes.

"Luke, you were a good soldier. You found Edward. You saved him, baby." Her eyes were glistening as tears of her own fell. The dark circles under them were highlighted by their gleam. As the sun finally rose from behind the ridge, Luke felt hope.

At the hospital, nurses swarmed around Eddie. The men who had carried him in the blanket from the forest to the house and from the house to the ambulance, had stuck by his side and reluctantly released their protective huddle. Luke looked over at his mother and grabbed her hand. They had followed the ambulance in the car and now waited patiently as the doctors and nurses wheeled Eddie through large white doors, away from the emergency lobby.

"He's goin' to be fine, Luke, baby. He's gonna be fine."

Luke couldn't tell if she was saying this more for his sake, or hers. At the moment, he didn't care. The pain in his head was unbearable, and his breathing still hadn't returned to normal. The wheezy goo still filtered each breath and the throbbing in his skull had not subsided. In fact, it grew more intense with each flimsy inhale.

His mother draped her arm across his shoulders and squeezed. "You look tired, baby. Why don't you get some sleep? Eddie's in good hands now." She sniffled and tapped a white tissue at the corners of her eyes. Luke heard her but he couldn't reply. Hammers had replaced his brain and were fighting their way to get out, or at least, that's what it felt like, so he nodded.

Stretching his legs out and turning so that his head lay in her lap, Luke fell asleep.

"W-what?" Edward's eyes fluttered open. "Where am I?"

His mother was at his side in an instant. Or he thought that it was his mom. He couldn't really see. Only one eye could open, and glory was it blurry. Her voice confirmed his assumption. "Oh, Eddie! Thank God! Thank God, you're awake!" She scooped up his hand and the heat that radiated off it felt good against Edward's skin. He was so cold.

He tried to speak again, but his throat protested. All that came out was a cough. Instantly, his mother pulled a cup from the side table and placed the straw to his lips. Edward pulled slowly, wincing as the icy liquid hit his throat. He tried once more to speak. "Where... am I?"

"You're at the hospital, baby. Your daddy will be here soon. I called him after..." Her voice caught and Edward noticed for the first time that she had been crying. Her free hand touched the tip of her nose. Edward knew that touch—that was the 'I don't want to cry again' touch. "He's goin' to be here soon."

"Where's Luke?"

"Oh, I carried him in here." She pointed to the couch. "He, bless his heart, he fell asleep out in the lobby. They," she sniffled, "they had you in surgery for eight hours... You, you'd been attacked."

Memories crashed over him then, each moment on a roulette wheel, spinning over and over again. The pain flashed across his body. He tried to move.

"Oh no, honey. Don't. Don't move. They had to reset your collarbone and you have a lot of stitches..."

Edward nodded and settled back into a statue-like state. His eyes scanned the room, settling on Luke's body. He studied it for a long time. His heart felt as if it could explode from the affection he felt towards that small, annoying boy. He wanted to talk to him. To tell him everything would be fine. Everything was always fine. They had each other's backs. They always did, no matter the game, no matter the struggle. They were brothers, and brothers stuck together.

"Can we wake him up?" Edward asked hoarsely.

"Yeah, I'll try to wake him. You want to talk to him?"

Edward nodded. He felt pricks at the inside corners of his eyes. He was safe. Luke was safe. All he needed now was to hear that small voice break the glass-like silence of the hospital. To disturb the repetitious beeping of monitors.

That's all. Then he'd go back to sleep and remove the exhaustion housing itself in his bones.

"Luke," she cooed, "Luke, Eddie's awake. He wants to talk to you." Luke didn't budge.

"Luke." She placed a hand on his shoulder. "Luke, wake up. Eddie wants to talk to you." His mother's hand moved to rub Luke's arm. As soon as it had settled, she stiffened. "Luke!" She shook him.

"Luke!" She shook him harder.

A chilled, silky feeling crawled over Edward. A hopeless, black entity. He watched as his mother's voice vanished even though her lips still moved. He watched as his brother's arm fell limply over the edge of the couch. He watched as she ran from the room, only to be followed back in by a white coat. He watched as the white coat picked up Luke's body and hauled him out of the room. He watched them leave him there, alone, with his thoughts. He watched and he knew.

Luke was gone.

A sharp shattering sensation settled over him. Pain, unlike that he had felt the night before, ripped through him. He'd heard people talk about it, but he'd never really believed it was real.

A broken heart.

"Nothing hurts worse than a broken heart," they had said. They were right.

When his ears finally had begun to listen once more; '*anyeurysm*' was what he pulled from the fog of voices.

Luke had had an aneurysm.

Ingram Content Group UK Ltd.
Milton Keynes UK
UKHW010748280423
420934UK00001B/127

9 781804 392027